Anansi Finds a Fool

AN ASHANTI TALE

Verna Aardema

pictures by Bryna Waldman

Dial Books for Young Readers ❉ *New York*

Published by Dial Books for Young Readers · A Division of Penguin Books USA Inc.
375 Hudson Street · New York, New York 10014

Text copyright © 1992 by Verna Aardema · Pictures copyright © 1992 by Bryna Waldman
Typography by Amelia Lau Carling · All rights reserved
Printed in Hong Kong by South China Printing Company (1988) Limited
First Edition
3 5 7 9 10 8 6 4

Library of Congress Cataloging in Publication Data
Aardema, Verna. Anansi finds a fool / by Verna Aardema ; pictures by Bryna Waldman.
p.   cm.
A retelling of Robert S. Rattray's story beginning on p. 253 in his book,
Akan-Ashanti folk-tales published by the Clarendon Press, Oxford, 1930.
Includes bibliographical references.
Summary: Lazy Anansi seeks to trick someone into doing the heavy work of
laying his fish trap, but instead he is fooled into doing the job himself.
ISBN 0-8037-1164-6 (trade).—ISBN 0-8037-1165-4 (library)
[1. Anansi (Legendary character) 2. Folklore—Africa, West.]
I. Waldman, Bryna, ill. II. Rattray, R.S. (Robert Sutherland), 1881–1938.
Akan-Ashanti folk-tales. III. Title.
PZ8. 1. A213An 1992   398.24'52544—dc20   [E]   91-21127   CIP   AC

Anansi Finds a Fool is an Ashanti tale, retold from a story by
Robert S. Rattray in *Akan-Ashanti Folk-tales*, Oxford at the Clarendon Press, 1930.

The art for this book was done with watercolors. The artwork
was then color-separated and reproduced in full color.

Glossary

Anansi (a-NAHN-see): Sometimes a spider and other times a man,
as in this tale. (West African folktales are called *Spider Stories*
whether Anansi appears in them or not.)

Ashanti (a-SHAHN-tee): Natives of Ghana (GAHN-a),
on the west coast of Africa

Aso (AH-so): Wife of Anansi, either in human or arachnid form

Bonsu (BON-soo): Anansi's fishing partner

Kiliwili (KEE-le-WEE-le): Ideophone meaning *headlong*

Laluah (LA-loo-ah): Wife of Bonsu

To my grandson, Damian Bullis,
who likes to go fishing.
V.A.

For Nicole and Chato
who have taught me a great deal. Thanks!
B.W.

In West Africa there once lived a man named Anansi. He was greedy and lazy and always up to some trick. One morning he announced to Aso, his wife, that he was going into the fishing business.

Aso said, "One of my ears has heard. There remains the other."

Anansi chuckled, *"Huh, huh, huh."* He said, "I'm going to find a fool for a partner—someone who will do all the work while I get all the fish."

"Ha!" said Aso. "Where will you find such a fool?" She put her water jar on her head and set out for the river.

At the riverside Aso met Laluah, the wife of Bonsu.

Laluah asked, "Are you well?"

"I am quite well," said Aso. "It's that husband of mine. He said he's going into the fishing business. And he's going to find a fool to help him—someone who will do all the work while he gets all the fish."

Laluah went home and told Bonsu what Aso had said.

Bonsu thought about that for a small time. Then he said, "I'll go fishing with Anansi. I will beat him at his own game!"

Bonsu went to Anansi's house. He said, "Anansi, I'll go fishing with you. Two can catch fish better than one."

Anansi was surprised at Bonsu's offer. And a little uncomfortable too. Bonsu would not be easy to trick. But he said, "All right. First we will have to make a fish trap."

Anansi and Bonsu went looking for material for the trap. They found some raffia palms. And Bonsu said, "Anansi, give me the knife. I'll cut the branches. And your part will be to get tired for me."

"Hold it, man," cried Anansi. "Why should I get tired for you?"

"When work is being done, someone has to get tired," said Bonsu. "If I cut the branches, the least you can do is to take the weariness."

Anansi said, "The tiredness is the worst part! I'll do the cutting myself. And YOU must get tired for ME!"

So Anansi climbed the raffia palm and began slashing off the fronds.

Bonsu sat nearby. And every time Anansi chopped, Bonsu grunted, "Kra…UNH, kra…UNH, kra…UNH!"

Soon there was a great pile of material cut.

Then Bonsu said, "Now you sit down, Anansi. I'll make the trap. Sore fingers and an aching back is what I'll get. But I will do the work, if you will suffer for me."

"Hold it, man," said Anansi. "You are doing fine taking the misery. I'll make the fish trap myself."

While Anansi worked, Bonsu suffered. He wiped his brow, rubbed his back, and moaned, *"Du, du, du."*

Bonsu's fussing was such a diversion that Anansi forgot his own discomfort. By weaving and tying, weaving and tying, he finally finished the trap.

"What a fine fish trap!" exclaimed Bonsu, as he balanced it on his head. "If we meet any people on the way to the river, they will think I made it."

"Wait," cried Anansi. "Why should you get the credit for my work?" And he pulled the trap off Bonsu's head and put it on his own.

When the two reached the riverside, Bonsu said, "Anansi, there are crocodiles in the river. Let me set the trap. If I get a leg bitten off, you can die for me."

"Hold it, man," cried Anansi. "Do you take me for a fool? I'll plant the trap myself. If a crocodile gets me, YOU can die for ME!"

Anansi carried the trap into a patch of water reeds near the shore. As he was tying it to a reed stem near the bottom of the river, his groping hand disturbed a crayfish.

Then *kapp!* A huge claw clamped on to his little finger.

"Waaaaaa!" yelled Anansi, as he came splashing out of the water—the crayfish dangling from his hand like a fish at the end of a fish pole.

Bonsu pried the claw off Anansi's finger.
Then he said, "This is the biggest crayfish
I have ever seen. It will make a fine meal for
you and Aso."

"You take it," said Anansi, as he wrapped
a leaf around his bleeding finger. "I'll get whatever is in the trap in the morning."

When Laluah saw the fine crayfish that
Bonsu had brought, she clapped her hands.
And immediately she put the kettle on to boil.

When Anansi arrived home, Aso said, "Well, how did it go?"

"How did what go?" asked Anansi. He was not anxious to tell her anything.

"The fishing business," said Aso.

Anansi said, "The trap is in the water. And whatever is in it in the morning will be all ours."

The next morning, as soon as the darkness was torn aside, Anansi and Bonsu went to look at their fish trap. As they reached the riverside, they saw that the reeds around the trap were agitated.

The two ran *kiliwili* down the bank into the river. They closed the large end of the trap and dragged it out of the water. It was heavy— full of something big and black and coiled! They set it down hastily and backed away.

Then *purup!* The flap on the trap burst open. And out slithered a huge python. Its body was a series of humps and bumps.

"Look!" cried Bonsu. "That snake has swallowed your fish! Count them!"

Anansi counted, "One, two, three, four..."

And by that time the python had dragged its loaded body *gu-bu-du* back into the river.

Anansi said, "Bonsu, you can't count that as my turn. I'll have whatever comes into the trap next. And we'll stay right here and watch."

The two men put the trap back into the river.

Time passed, time passed, time passed. At last they heard the *swop* of a fish jumping in the water.

Suddenly *swop…swop…swop!* The river was full of apopokiki fish leaping in and out of the water—all heading upstream.

Anansi jumped up and began yelling to the fish, "Into the trap! Go into the trap!"

"A crocodile is chasing them!" cried Bonsu.

Then *whoosh!* The fish trap rose up out of the water, spilling fish and revealing the head of a crocodile inside it!

The crocodile thrashed this way and that, trying to shake off the frightening hat. Then it came lumbering up out of the water.

Anansi shinnied up one tree; and Bonsu another. From the trees they watched the crocodile bash their trap against the ground, *BAKATAK! BAKATAK!* Finally it fell away. And the crocodile sashayed back into the water and streaked off after the school of apopokiki.

Anansi and Bonsu climbed down and examined the trap.

Bonsu said, "Sorry, my friend. The trap is finished. But it still does not look too bad. I think I shall take it to the market and sell it."

"Hold it, man," said Anansi. "I didn't get one lone fish from this fishing business—not even a crayfish. And now you want to take the trap away from me! I'll take it and sell it myself."

Anansi took the trap to the market. He sat down beside it and called out, "Fish trap for sale. Fish trap for sale."

People saw that the trap was badly broken. They told the headman of the village.

The headman went to Anansi and said, "Do you think that my people are so ignorant that they will buy a good-for-nothing fish trap? You insult us!"

Then he made Anansi put the trap on his head and walk through the market, crying, "No-good fish trap for sale. No-good fish trap for sale."

Anansi's eyes died for shame. The people howled with laughter. And children followed him shouting, *"Nah! Nah! Nah!"*

When it was over, Bonsu came to him and said, "Anansi, you were looking for a fool to go fishing with. You didn't have far to look. You were the fool yourself."

Anansi said, "But, Bonsu, what kind of a partner were you? When all of those people were making fun of me, at least you should have taken the shame!"

The next morning Aso and Laluah met again at the river. They saw the flattened water reeds and the trampled shore—the aftermath of their husbands' fishing business.

And when Laluah told Aso how Bonsu had tricked Anansi into doing all the work, Aso laughed so hard, the water jar slipped off her head.

As she caught it, Aso said, "It's a true saying: When you dig a hole for someone else, you will fall into it yourself."